Rock & Roll!

BOOK 15

BY
DOTTI ENDERLE

ILLUSTRATED BY
HOWARD MCWILLIAM

magic
wagon

Printed in the United States of America, North Mankato, MN.
102013
012014

 This book contains at least 10% recycled materials.

Text by Dotti Enderle
Illustrations by Howard McWilliam
Edited by Stephanie Hedlund and Rochelle Baltzer
Cover and interior design by Jaime Martens

Library of Congress Cataloging-in-Publication Data

Enderle, Dotti, 1954- author.
  Rock & roll! / by Dotti Enderle ; illustrated by Howard McWilliam.
    pages cm. -- (Ghost detectors ; book 15)
  Summary: When the ghost of a rock star interferes with a music
concert that Dandy, Malcolm, and his sister Cocoa are attending,
the ghost detectors are on the job--but this time the key to victory
may be a video game.
  ISBN 978-1-62402-003-2
1. Ghost stories. 2. Guitarists--Juvenile fiction. 3. Video games--
Juvenile fiction. 4. Brothers and sisters--Juvenile fiction. 5. Best
friends--Juvenile fiction. 6. Humorous stories. [1. Ghosts--Fiction.
2. Video games--Fiction. 3. Brothers and sisters--Fiction. 4. Best
friends--Fiction. 5. Friendship--Fiction. 6. Humorous stories.] I.
McWilliam, Howard, 1977- illustrator. II. Title. III. Title: Rock and
roll. IV. Series: Enderle, Dotti, 1954- Ghost Detectors ; bk.15.
  PZ7.E69645Ro 2014
  813.6--dc23
                                        2013025334

Contents

The King of Rock

Malcolm yelled, "I'm terrible at this!" No matter how fast his fingers slid up and down on the neck of the plastic guitar, he just couldn't keep up with the blaring rock song.

Whose stupid idea was it to give him a Rock Like a Star video game for his birthday anyway? Oh yeah . . . his dad's. The guy loved that old geezer music.

His best friend Dandy's fingers flew over the frets of his red guitar. His score

was three times higher than Malcolm's. Dandy really knew how to rock.

Malcolm sighed. "I give up." He set his blue guitar down and plopped onto the couch.

Dandy still stood, legs slightly apart, twanging along with the video game. He chewed his tongue as he concentrated. And he barely blinked his eyes. His score rolled higher . . . and higher . . . and higher. With a huge blast, the song finally ended. Dandy held his arms up in a victory *V*.

"I am the King of Rock!"

"Wow!" Malcolm couldn't believe it. Dandy had scored over 95,000 points. Far better than the lousy 20,000 he'd scored. "You're really good at this."

"What can I say?" Dandy wiggled his fingers in front of his face. "I've got the magic touch."

"You can play it any time you want," Malcolm said. "It's not really my kind of game."

"Thanks," Dandy beamed, trying to put his guitar down. The strap got caught on his ear. When he turned the controller around to pop it loose, some of the buttons got caught in his hair. "I'm sorry you didn't get the video game you wanted," he said as he tried to untwist the gadget.

Malcolm was sorry, too. He'd asked for Ghost Stalkers—the Home Game. It was based on his favorite reality TV show. In the game, the players try to detect famous ghosts and zap them with lasers. Malcolm knew he could score high on that one. Ghost detecting and zapping were his specialties.

"I never asked for Rock Like a Star. I think my dad wanted it," Malcolm said.

Dandy still struggled to get his hair loose from the controller. He gave new meaning to the phrase "plucking a guitar."

"Parents are like that sometimes," Dandy said. "For my birthday, my mom gave me a DVD of *Medical Miracles*, season one. I don't even like that show. And she only watches it because she thinks one of the actors is dreamy. She gets all giggly and gaga when he's on." Dandy made goo-goo eyes to imitate her.

"I know which actor you're talking about," Malcolm said. "Every time they show him, Grandma Eunice nearly jumps out of her wheelchair. She whistles and hoots and yells things like, 'He's hotter than a jalapeño on a grilled-cheese sandwich!'"

The more Dandy tried to free his hair, the more it got caught in the buttons.

HIGH SCORE
95,630

"Maybe on their birthdays we should give our parents what *we* want."

"That's a good idea." Malcolm looked back at the TV. Dandy's super high score flashed in neon colors while a crowd of cheering video fans still squealed and applauded. Dandy was definitely the King of Rock.

Just then he heard a ripping noise followed by "Ow!" He turned back to Dandy. The King of Rock now had a bald spot on the side of his head.

Dandy held up the red guitar and grinned. "Want to play again?"

Lou-Ny-Ben

Malcolm and Dandy played the game three more times. Each time, Dandy breezed through, scoring big. Malcolm slunk like a mouse, barely getting by. His highest score came when he imagined the musical notes were evil spirits that he—*whap!*—sent flying off the stage. But even those scores weren't all that great.

When it was time for Dandy to leave, he did the *V* arms again. "From now on,

I'm the King of Rock!"

Malcolm rolled his eyes. "Are you going to tell people that it was your adoring fans that ripped out a hunk of your hair?"

Dandy's hand flew up to the bald spot. "Maybe I can shave a design into it."

"Or cover it with your Rock Star crown."

Dandy nodded. "That's not a bad idea."

"That's a terrible idea, Dandy."

"Yeah, I guess you're right." But he still seemed to be gloating over his Rock Like a Star talent. "Later," he said as he strutted out the door.

Malcolm packed the video game back into the box. "Much later."

He'd barely closed the lid when his

sister, Cocoa, stormed in. "Mom! Mom!"

She was dressed in a tangerine-colored shirt, lemon-yellow striped skirt, and purple ankle boots. The boots matched the lavender streaks in her hair.

"What's wrong?" Malcolm asked. "Fashion disaster?"

She stomped over and pinched him with her raspberry-colored nails. "The only disaster will be what I do to you if you don't hush."

"Ow!" He rubbed his arm.

"Mom! Mom!" she screamed again.

Malcolm's mom peeked her head around a door. They'd both learned a long time ago that Cocoa's shrieks were never an emergency.

"What is it?" his mom asked.

Cocoa bounced on her toes with excitement. "I need eighty-five dollars."

"Ha!" Malcolm said.

Cocoa scowled at him. "Shut it!"

Their mom stepped in. "Why on earth do you need eighty-five dollars?"

Cocoa continued to bounce. "You're not going to believe this."

Malcolm bounced on his toes while clapping his hands. "You're going to buy a one-way bus ticket to the loony bin?"

"Yes!" she answered, clapping her hands.

Wait . . . what? "You're really going to the loony bin?"

She was practically springing out of her

ankle boots. "If Mom gives me eighty-five dollars."

Malcolm spun around to face his mom. "Quick! Give it to her. She could be out of here before dinner. I'll even help her pack." It was a dream come true!

A couch pillow came flying and hit Malcolm in the back of the head. He turned to Cocoa, who stood with her hands on her hips. "Not that kind of loony bin, you dummy. I'm talking about the boy band, Lou-Ny-Ben. They're coming to Castle Arena."

Oh yeah. They were three guys who became instant idols when they performed on a major reality talent show. Cocoa nearly burned up her speed dial voting for them. But Malcolm thought they looked goofy, danced funny, and had too much gel in their hair. And most of the lyrics

to their songs were just three words—girl, baby, and ooh.

"Please, Mom, please!" Cocoa begged.

Their mom crossed her arms. "I don't know. Eighty-five dollars is a lot of money."

Cocoa clasped her hands, pleading. "But Lou-Ny-Ben is worth every dime. Pleeeease?"

"Okay," their mom said. "When do tickets go on sale?"

Cocoa was boinging up and down like a wacky jack-in-the-box. "Tomorrow morning!" She flew across the room, flung her arms around their mom, and chanted, "Thank you! Thank you! Thank you! You're the best mom in the world."

"You're welcome," Malcolm's mom

said, prying Cocoa away. "But if you don't clean your room, I might change my mind."

"I'm on it." Cocoa danced down the hall, singing a Lou-Ny-Ben song.

"Mom?" Malcolm asked.

His mom picked up the couch pillow and placed it back in its spot. "Yes?"

"Can I have eighty-five dollars?"

She tilted her head toward him. "You want to go see Lou-Ny-Ben too?"

Malcolm cringed. "Ugh. No. I want to buy the Ghost Stalkers' home game."

His mom looked at him, puzzled. "But we just bought you a video game."

He pointed to the box. "It turns out, I'm not much of a rock star."

His mom patted his shoulder. "You just

need to practice. Get your dad to help. He loves that old music. Besides, those ghosts in that Stalkers game might give you nightmares."

If she only knew the truth! Malcolm thought.

Let's Trade

The next morning, Dandy sat next to Malcolm in the backseat of Malcolm's mom's car. Cocoa was in the front passenger seat, singing along with some Lou-Ny-Ben song streaming through her earbuds. They were cruising on their way to buy Cocoa her concert ticket.

As far as Malcolm was concerned, they couldn't get there fast enough. Cocoa sounded like a cat caught in a clothes dryer.

"Why are we tagging along?" Dandy whispered as he adjusted the baseball cap he had on to hide his bald spot. On the front he'd written KOR with a black marker. *KOR* for "King of Rock." And to look super cool, he was wearing it backward.

The bill on the cap kept knocking against the seat, causing the cap to pop up and down. He looked like a PEZ candy dispenser. "We're not buying tickets."

Malcolm raised an eyebrow. "Because I have a plan."

Dandy turned toward Malcolm. But his cap didn't. It sat sideways on his head. "What's the plan?"

Malcolm hunkered, speaking low. "The ticket counter at the mall is next door to Games Aflame. I'm going to talk my mom

into taking us in there and buying the Ghost Stalkers game."

"How are you going to do that?"

Malcolm scratched his head. "I haven't figured that part out yet."

When they turned into the mall parking lot, they all gawked. "My goodness," Malcolm's mom said. "This is a circus."

The place was packed. There were reporters from the local newspaper and TV station. A van from the radio station, Party Pop 9.5, was there, complete with flashing red and gold lights and music blaring through a giant speaker.

A line of girls about Cocoa's age wrapped halfway around the mall. They were holding banners and posters that said things like, *Lou-Ny-Ben Fever!* and *Lou-Ny-Ben Maniacs.*

Malcolm rolled his eyes. "They're maniacs, all right," he murmured to Dandy.

His mom found a parking spot way in the back corner, and they wormed their way through the parked cars toward the long ticket line.

As they were passing the Party Pop radio van, a man with spiked hair, checkered shoes, and a long, skinny microphone jumped out at them.

"Aaaah!" Dandy yelled, as the guy snatched him by the arm and pulled him up onto a small platform. Malcolm recognized the guy. He was the nighttime DJ, Curly Cue.

"Ho!" Curly said, shoving the microphone in front of Dandy's face. "What's your name, fellow?"

Dandy's eyes crossed as he looked at

the microphone almost touching his nose. "Uh . . . Dandy."

"Dandy!" the DJ yelled. "Can we all give Dandy a Party Pop hello?"

A small crowd of kids put their fingers in their mouths and went *pop!* Dandy *popped* back.

"Nice hat," Curly said. He spun Dandy around. "What does KOR stand for?"

Dandy grinned. "King of Rock."

"Whoa! Folks, we have the King of Rock here." He snatched the cap off Dandy's head.

Dandy quickly slapped his hand to his head to hide the bald spot. Too late. Curly pointed at it. "And he's the King of Punk, too!"

Malcolm wondered if he should jump up there and rescue Dandy. Curly was being a real sleazeball.

Curly fanned himself with Dandy's cap. "Tell you what," he said. "How about I trade you?"

Dandy's face pinched. "Trade?"

Curly leaned lower. The microphone nearly went up Dandy's nose. "You let me keep this cap, and I'll give you four front-row seats to Lou-Ny-Ben."

Dandy gulped. "But I like that cap."

He didn't get to say much else because Cocoa flew up onto the tiny stage and jammed the cap onto Curly's head. "It's a deal!"

Curly's eyes bulged and his hair grew even spikier. Malcolm knew that kind of fear. Curly whipped out the tickets and shoved them and the cap at Dandy. "Enjoy the show."

Cocoa threw her arms around Curly and gave him a big kiss on the cheek. "We will." Then she grabbed Dandy by his sleeve and jerked him down with her.

She rubbed her palms together and licked her lips. "Thanks, Dandy." Then looking up to the sky, she shouted, "Yes! I have front-row seats!"

Dandy glared down at the tickets, then

at Cocoa. "No, you don't. He gave them to me."

Cocoa froze. Her face turned spinach green. "But I'm the Lou-Ny-Ben fan, not you."

Dandy shrugged. "I like them pretty good. And it'll be fun to sit in the front row."

Cocoa gritted her teeth so hard it sounded like she was biting gravel. "But you're going to share, right?"

Malcolm's mom stepped between them. "Remember, Dandy, you wouldn't have those tickets if it weren't for Cocoa."

She was right. Dandy was only tagging

along. And he knew it. He handed two of the tickets to Cocoa. "We'll split them."

"Yes!" She did a dance that looked like a cross between a sailor's jig and a monkey scratching an itch.

"Great," their mom said. "Now we can leave."

Malcolm panicked. "But I wanted to go into Games Aflame."

His mom looked around at the crowd. "Maybe next weekend."

Sigh.

Show's Cancelled

If there was one thing that made Malcolm's skin crawl, it was hearing Cocoa squeal. *Ugh!* But now he sat in an echoing auditorium filled with 20,000 squealing girls. *Double ugh!* He should've brought earmuffs!

"I can't believe we came to this!" he yelled to Dandy. "I don't even like Lou-Ny-Ben!"

Dandy had his KOR cap swiveled on backward again. A girl behind him kept

knocking it with her *Got Lou-Ny-Ben?* poster.

"I don't like them either," he yelled back to Malcolm.

"Then why are we here?"

"'Cause I've never been in the front row before."

Malcolm looked behind him at the sea of girls bouncing on the seats, hopping in the air and wailing like they'd just won a million dollars. "And it looks like this is the safest spot."

He glanced at Cocoa. She was practically doing cartwheels. She jumped and hollered as she tugged on her blue Lou-Ny-Ben T-shirt. It was tucked into the red plastic skirt she wore over pink paisley leggings and gravy-colored platform shoes.

"If she's this bad now," Dandy said, "what do you think it'll be like when the band comes onstage?"

As batty as Cocoa was acting, Malcolm knew she could kick it up three more notches. "Brace yourself," he told Dandy.

Minutes later, the lights dimmed. Spotlights circled the auditorium. Then Party Pop's main man, Curly Cue, jogged onto the stage. Dandy clutched his cap.

Curly grabbed the microphone. "Are you ready?"

Malcolm rolled his eyes. These girls had practically clawed the seats apart. They were definitely ready.

A wave of shouts rolled up, making his ears ring. "Yes!"

Curly leaned toward the crowd like he couldn't hear. "I said, are you ready?!"

This time, Malcolm was. He and Dandy both covered their ears.

"Yes!!!"

"Then here they are. Lou . . . Ny . . . Ben!"

Curly ran off as the three boy singers swaggered onto the stage. They winked and waved as they went to their mikes. Then they jumped into their number one hit, singing, "Ooh Girl, You're My Baby, Ooh."

Girls were howling, sobbing, and hugging each other. Their dream come true was Malcolm's nightmare. He'd rather face an army of vicious ghosts.

But right then, something weird happened. Ny—or as Cocoa called him, "the cute one"—froze. His eyes bugged and his hair stood straight up.

Lou and Ben kept singing, but they threw sideways glares at him. Then Ny rose about a foot in the air and started spinning like a whirligig. The other two guys jumped back, their eyes wide as moons.

The crowd thought it was part of the show. They cheered and shouted, "Spin, Ny, spin!"

But Lou, the dreamy one, rushed over to help. He grabbed hold of Ny's feet. Soon he was winding round and round, looking like a human crank.

Ben, the smart one, stayed back.

The prerecorded music belched to a stop. So did Lou and Ny. They staggered around for a moment, then threw up all over the stage. The crowd went quiet. Then there was a collective sound of *Ewwww.* There's nothing cute or dreamy about puke.

Curly Cue ran onto the stage, but just as he grabbed the microphone, new music blared over the speakers. Malcolm looked at Dandy. Dandy looked at Malcolm. *Huh?*

"What's that?" Dandy asked.

Malcolm shrugged. "I don't know. But I intend to find out."

The Drill Bit Curse!

Malcolm and Dandy went home and headed straight to Malcolm's basement lab. They sat pretzel-style on the floor while Malcolm powered up his laptop. In a search engine, he typed *drill bit curse*. Up popped dozens of links. All of them were about the Drill Bits' last gig at Castle Arena.

"Wow!" Malcolm said. "Can you believe this?" He read part of an article: "On August 22, 1989, during their concert

here, the Drill Bits' lead guitarist, Amp Tracer, was electrocuted while strumming his guitar with his tongue. He danced around with sparks flying for a whole minute before anyone realized it wasn't part of the act. Cal Cannon, the Drill Bits' drummer said, 'We tried to help him, but the stage was sticky from the fog machine fumes. We kept slipping and falling.' Once the fog had cleared, one bystander described Amp as 'a fried egg with a side of hash browns.'"

Below the article was a photo of Amp Tracer wearing tight leopard print pants tucked into black knee boots. His T-shirt had so many rips and holes it reminded Malcolm of the ones his mom used as soap rags. His long, shaggy hair feathered around him, and he held a spotted snake.

Dandy's eyes bulged. "I guess that was a cool look back then."

"For rock stars," Malcolm added.

Dandy nodded. "I can't believe he died right there on the stage. It must've been shocking for his fans."

Malcolm couldn't resist saying it. "More shocking for him." He pointed back to the computer screen. "But look at this. There have been at least ten other incidences at Castle Arena like what happened tonight. Singers and musicians are either hurt or run off the stage. And every time, the song 'Unraveled' starts to play."

"That must have been the song that they were playing when he got jolted," Dandy said.

"Probably," Malcolm agreed. "But I think what happened tonight was more than a curse."

"Do you think Amp's ghost is hanging out there?" Dandy asked.

Malcolm tapped his chin. "Yeah. But we need to examine the footage."

Dandy lifted his cap and scratched his bald spot. "What footage?"

"The footage on Cocoa's phone."

If there was one thing Malcolm hated, it was asking Cocoa for a favor. He and Dandy tiptoed to her room. "Shhh," Malcolm warned as he gently knocked.

"Who is it?" Cocoa screeched.

Malcolm quietly eased open the door.

"Get out!" she yelled.

Malcolm carefully stepped into her room. He could see that Cocoa was crying. Well, it was more like blubbering. Her face was blotchy, her nose was lobster red, and black streaks of eye makeup tracked down her cheeks. *Yikes!* But he knew the only way to get that video was to be nice.

"Cocoa, I'm really sorry about what happened at the concert. I know how much you were looking forward to seeing Lou-Ny-Ben."

Cocoa stopped sobbing and gave him the stink eye. "What do you care? You didn't even want to be there."

"But you did," he said nicely. "And I feel really bad that you weren't able to enjoy a full hour and a half of their great music."

Cocoa went back to wailing.

Dandy cowered behind as Malcolm crept a little closer. "It just isn't fair."

Cocoa tilted her head and narrowed her eyes. "You want something. I can tell."

Busted! Oh well. "I just want to borrow your phone for about five minutes."

"Use your own phone." She threw one of her ruffled pillows at him.

"I don't have one," he said, batting the pillow away. "Mom says I have to wait until I'm in middle school."

"Then use the house phone, dork."

"Truthfully, I need to see that video you took," he admitted.

She sneered at him. "Why, so you can make fun of it?"

"I want to analyze it," he told her. "I think there was some kind of mechanical failure. If I can point it out to the stage managers, I bet Lou-Ny-Ben will be back before you know it."

She gave him a blank stare. "If it was a mechanical failure, the stage people will find it without your help."

Malcolm slumped. If she didn't hand it over, he'd have to wait till she was asleep and sneak it away. He didn't want to wait that long. He was about to start begging when Dandy stepped in front of him.

"Give us the phone," Dandy ordered.

"No way, baldy," Cocoa snarked.

"I gave you two of my free tickets," he said. "You owe me."

"Do not."

"Do too."

She placed her hands on her hips. "You only got them because we drove you there."

"I got them because I'm the King of Rock." He turned around and pointed to the KOR on his cap. "Curly wanted my cap, remember?"

Malcolm couldn't believe it. He'd never seen Dandy act this brave.

"Five minutes," she said, slapping it into Dandy's hand. "If I don't have it back by then, you're dead meat."

"Thanks!" Malcolm said as they raced out the door.

"And you better not prank call any of my friends," she shouted after them.

Any other time, that might be fun, but right now, the last thing Malcolm cared about was calling Cocoa's friends.

Rock & Roll Grandma?

Malcolm plugged the phone into his computer. A few seconds later, the video was his. Dandy raced upstairs to give Cocoa back her phone with four minutes to spare. Once he returned, they played the footage.

Cocoa had started filming while Ny was spinning. He helicoptered for a few seconds before Lou grabbed his ankles. It was like a boy band tornado.

"Look!" Malcolm blurted.

Just as Lou and Ny hurled their dinner all over the stage, there was a weird glitch.

"What?" Dandy asked. "I didn't see anything."

Malcolm played it again. "There." He clicked pause.

Dandy leaned close to the screen. "Holy cow!"

Right above the barfing boys was the ghostly image of Amp Tracer.

"I knew it," Malcolm said.

"But why?" Dandy wondered. "Why would Amp ruin the concert?"

Malcolm shrugged. "Whatever the reason, we have to stop him. No one wants to see a boy band upchuck on stage."

Dandy nodded. "Especially from the front row!"

Malcolm tapped his chin, thinking. "We need a plan."

"It's simple," Dandy said. "We just go back to Castle Arena and zap him."

"That's easy enough. The hard part is figuring out how to get in."

"Can't we buy a ticket to the next show?" Dandy asked.

Malcolm clicked on the schedule for upcoming events. "The next show is a ballet called *Swan Lake*."

"You're right," Dandy said. "We need a plan."

Just then, they heard the echoes of a rock song playing.

Malcolm tilted his head to listen. "Wait. Isn't that 'Unraveled'?"

Dandy nodded, eyes wide. "That's it

all right."

"Where's it coming from?" Malcolm whispered.

Dandy looked like he was two beats away from running for dear life. His lips were ice blue. "Do you think Amp followed us home?"

Malcolm took a deep breath. "Ghost hunters do attract ghosts."

The music seemed to be getting louder. Malcolm clicked on his Ecto-Handheld-Automatic-Heat-Sensitive-Laser-Enhanced Specter Detector. If Amp was here, it would save them the trouble of sneaking back into the arena. But the only ghost that appeared was Malcolm's pet dog, Spooky. *Yip! Yip!*

Malcolm placed a finger to his lips. "Shhh!"

The dog obeyed.

"I still hear the music," Dandy said. He trembled like jelly in an earthquake.

Malcolm pointed at the basement ceiling. "It's coming from upstairs."

Dandy grabbed Malcolm's ghost zapper and they crept up the stairs and out into the hallway. Dandy kept one hand on Malcolm's shoulder as they padded quietly toward the living room. Malcolm peeked around the corner and . . . "Grandma!"

Grandma Eunice was in front of the TV, strumming the red plastic guitar and rocking out to Rock Like a Star. "Woo-hoo! I'm the Queen of Rock!"

Malcolm looked at her score—125,000 points. Better than Dandy's! He slumped. *I'd have been happier if it had been Amp's ghost,* he thought.

My Favorite Song

Malcolm and Dandy hung back, peeking around at the back door of Castle Arena. There was a lot of hustling and bustling going on.

"They must have moved the Lou-Ny-Ben equipment out last night," Malcolm said. "The ballet people are already setting up."

There were several trucks and vans parked in the back alley. One van had

Romantic Moves Ballet Company written on the side.

"There are bunches of people scooting around," Dandy pointed out. "I bet we could get inside without anyone noticing."

"I think you're right," Malcolm agreed.

Dandy adjusted his KOR cap, Malcolm heaved his backpack (ghost detector and zapper inside), and they both strutted forward like they belonged there. But as they approached the back door, a security guard stepped in front of them. He crossed his arms and glared down.

"Where do you think you're going?"

Gulp! Malcolm pointed to his backpack. "Uh . . . I'm bringing the glue for the feathers. Those dancers can't be swans without feathers."

The security guard nodded.

Great! He's going to let us in, Malcolm thought.

But he pointed to the Romantic Moves van instead. "Give it to one of those folks over there. Someone will take it inside."

"It might be faster if we go," Malcolm said.

"Nah." The guard shook his head. "It's like a mob scene in there. You might get trampled."

"We're pretty good at dodging," Dandy bragged.

The guard didn't budge. "Can't have you underfoot."

"Thanks," Malcolm said, even though the guard hadn't done anything helpful. The boys went back to their lookout spot.

"Now what?" Dandy asked.

Malcolm waited and watched. The scenery was being hauled inside. There was a nighttime backdrop with lots of stars and a full moon and a daytime backdrop with billowy clouds and a yellow sun. There were large, sleek mirrors that looked like water. There were even a couple of wooden boats. But then he saw a chance.

"Look," he told Dandy. Malcolm pointed to one of the vans. The double doors in back of it were open, and a woman was pushing a rack down a ramp. The rack was crammed tight with costumes. "That's how we'll sneak in."

Dandy blinked. "I don't get it."

Malcolm motioned with his hand. "Don't worry. Just follow me."

They raced across the alley and hid behind the side of the van. The woman who had pushed the wardrobe rack down

stopped, snapped her fingers like she'd forgotten something, and then climbed back inside.

"Now," Malcolm said.

Dandy followed as Malcolm crept over, pushed aside some of the fluffy costumes, and scrunched between them.

"Are you in?" he whispered to Dandy.

"Uh-huh," Dandy whispered back. "But these ballerina costumes sure are scratchy."

Yep. Malcolm didn't know how those dancers flitted about in layers and layers of stiff netting. It felt like his face was being scrubbed with burnt toast.

He heard the lady coming back down the ramp. "Get ready to march," he whispered to Dandy. A few seconds later, the lady started pushing.

Malcolm held on to the sleeves of a leotard as he put one foot in front of the other. One slip and he might fall, bringing half the swan costumes down with him. They paced through the alley, up to the doors.

Uh-oh. Another ramp. He hung on for dear life as they trudged their way up. The

lady kept making weird grunting noises, but soon they were walking naturally. And they were inside!

They stayed hidden in the wardrobe rack till it came to a stop. Malcolm peered out. It looked like they'd been left alone in a dark closet.

"Let's get out of here," he said.

The boys wasted no time pushing their way out and rushing to the closet door. Malcolm slung it open, and they ran past a bunch of ballerinas doing stretches.

"The sound booth," Malcolm called back to Dandy. They hurried to the stairway and gobbled the steps two at a time. Once they were in the sound booth, Malcolm slumped down to the floor, panting. Then he looked around. *Gah!* "Dandy!"

Dandy looked at his reflection in the

sound booth window. "Ahhhh!" he howled. Around his jeans he was wearing a fluffy white tutu with glittery sparkles. On his cap rested a diamond tiara.

Malcolm grinned. "You look like a fairy princess."

"Hush," Dandy said, stripping the girly stuff off as quickly as he could.

Malcolm unzipped his backpack. "Time to get down to business." He pulled out his ghost detector and powered it up. "Okay, Amp. Where are you?"

A few seconds later, the electronic soundboard lit up. A few switches flipped, and the song "Unraveled" blared through the auditorium.

Amp suddenly appeared, leaning against the wall. "Ah . . . my favorite song."

Amp's Story

Malcolm rushed to the soundboard and shut off the music. He could see a crowd of people far below, peering up.

"Sorry," he said over the loudspeaker. "Wrong music."

The curious people went about their business. Malcolm stomped over to Amp, but not too close. The rocker was dressed in those same tight pants and boots. And that snake was coiled around his arm.

Malcolm wasn't sure if a ghost snake would strike, but he didn't want to find out.

"You can't keep doing this," he said to Amp.

Amp grinned. "I have to keep the Drill Bit Curse alive."

"But people pay lots of money to see the shows here. They want to enjoy themselves, not listen to some old song from a million years ago."

"Come on, 1989 was not that long ago," Amp argued.

"To you!" Malcolm shot back.

Dandy scooted closer to Malcolm. "Zap him," he whispered.

Amp's eyes almost doubled in size. His ghostly face grew even whiter. "I've been zapped before. Believe me, it's no fun." He opened his mouth wide and stuck out his blackened tongue. "See what happens when you're zapped?"

Malcolm didn't dare tell him that his zapper would do a lot more damage.

"I don't know how you could play a guitar with your tongue," Dandy said.

"Wouldn't those strings slice into it? And what about all those gross germs?"

"I always played the guitar that way. It was part of the show." He stuck out his nasty black tongue again and wiggled it like the snake on his arm. "The fans love it."

"Not anymore," Malcolm said.

Amp wilted a bit. "You're right. But music today is terrible. Boy bands, hip-hop, songs produced electronically. And sound effects! Today's music is filled with air horns, sirens, and auto-tuners. Who wants to sound like a robot?"

Dandy shrugged. "I think it's pretty cool."

Amp sneered. "Nobody asked you, Core."

Core?

"Think about it this way," Malcolm said to Amp. "How would you have liked it if someone had turned on pop music and spun you around the way you twirled Ny?"

"No one would've done that because I was the greatest."

The snake on his arm flicked its forked tongue like it was agreeing.

"You *were* the greatest," Dandy argued.

Amp yawned. "I'm bored." He pointed toward the soundboard and "Unraveled" blasted through the speakers again. Malcolm rushed over and shut it off.

"Sorry," he said again through the mike. "I accidentally hit the wrong button." He whipped around to Amp. "I'm bored too." He pulled out his zapper. "It's time to turn you into goo." As he pressed the button,

Amp faded away. The zapper juice hit the sound booth window and oozed down the glass.

Amp reappeared on the other side. "Bad shot." He pointed to Dandy. "Maybe you should let Core try."

"Why do you keep calling him Core?" Malcolm asked.

Amp circled his finger, spinning Dandy's cap frontward. "That's his name, isn't it? K.O.R. Kor?"

"That's not my name," Dandy said. "It's my title."

Amp raised a phantom eyebrow. "Your title?"

"Yeah," Dandy beamed. "I'm the King of Rock."

Amp's feathery hair stood up as his face turned tomato red. "Impossible. *I* am the

King of Rock."

Dandy shrugged. "Not anymore."

"Noooo!!!" Amp raised his arms. The soundboard lit up. "Unraveled" and four other Drill Bits songs began playing all at once. The music screamed through Malcolm's ears. He tried to turn it off, but the levels and switches kept moving up and down on their own.

The snake coiled around Amp's neck as the old rocker yelled, "I. Am. The. King. Of. Rock!"

He whisked around, his hands circling as he played air guitar. He bent into a lunging position, his fingers flying up and down imaginary frets. As he rocked out on his invisible instrument, he flicked his charcoal-black tongue.

There were shouts coming from below. Malcolm had to act quickly. He dropped

down to his knees, crawled under the soundboard, and pulled the electrical plug. The lights dimmed and the music slowed to a stop.

But Amp didn't stop. He kept swinging and swaying, making waa-waa noises like the twang of a guitar.

Malcolm and Dandy stood and watched.

"He's got some crazy moves," Dandy said.

"Yep," Malcolm agreed. "Crazy."

Amp finally clamped his eyes shut, leaped into the air, and came down in the splits. He held his arms up in victory. "I am the King of Rock!"

Dandy took off his cap and scratched his bald spot. "Dude, you don't even have a real guitar."

Amp pulled himself up off the floor. "Yeah, it exploded during the power surge."

"So you know what that means?" Dandy said.

Amp waited for the answer.

Dandy put his cap back on frontward. "You can't be the King of Rock unless you have a guitar."

Amp stomped his foot like a spoiled child. "I am so the King of Rock! I am!"

"There's only one way to settle this," Malcolm said.

Dandy, Amp, and the snake turned and looked at him.

Malcolm grinned. "Battle of the rock stars."

Amp narrowed his eyes. "You want me to compete against this little pipsqueak?"

Dandy stood taller, proud. "Let's do it."

Amp placed his hands on his hips and leaned close. "Whenever you're ready."

Malcolm stepped between them. "My basement. Tonight." He heaved his backpack up onto his shoulders. "We'll have two guitars ready and waiting."

Battle of the Rock Stars

Malcolm plugged Rock Like a Star into the small television in the basement.

"Let's make sure it's working," he told Dandy.

They each picked up a plastic guitar and strummed away. Dandy scored big. Malcolm ignored his total.

I'm getting worse at this, he thought.

"Okay," he clapped Dandy on the back. "Are you ready?"

Dandy scratched his bald spot, then put his King of Rock cap back on his head. "Ready to rock."

Malcolm took out his ghost detector and powered it up. Amp Tracer suddenly appeared, sitting cross-legged on the counter. "Waiting for me?" he asked.

"Yep," Malcolm answered. "You are going down, fellow!"

Amp rolled his eyes. "We'll see about that."

He hopped off the counter and strutted over to where the boys stood. His tight leopard print pants made a whooshing noise with each step. "Ready to rock?"

Dandy turned his cap frontward to show off his title. "Let's do this."

Malcolm held up both guitars. "Take your pick."

Amp looked at them, then his face pinched. "Really? We're going to jam out on these silly things? Ridiculous."

"Are you chickening out?" Dandy asked. "'Cause that means I stay the King of Rock."

"I'm not chicken!" He snatched up the red controller. Dandy took the blue one.

"Wait," Malcolm said, stepping between the two rockers and the TV. He leaned toward Amp. "If you win, you will stay the King of Rock, and we'll leave you alone."

Then he narrowed his eyes. "But if you lose that title, you have to stay away from Castle Arena. No more haunting. No more blaring your music. And no more

making boy bands puke onstage."

"Agreed," Amp said.

The two competitors got ready to rock. Dandy spread his legs in a power stance. Amp bent into a lunging position. Then Malcolm turned on "Unraveled" and stepped out of the way. The battle was on.

Dandy's score counter was rolling up . . . up . . . up. It looked like he might break his own record. But wait. Amp was racking up points, too. Big points!

How is that possible? Malcolm asked himself. There's no way Amp could've played this game before. But the guy was totally killing it.

Halfway through the song, Amp had jumped ahead. He was 9,000 points above Dandy. Malcolm started to sweat. "Go,

Dandy, go!"

Dandy's fingers were flying over the buttons, but he missed several notes now and then. Amp hit almost every one.

"I've got this," Dandy assured Malcolm. He leaned into a lunging position, just like Amp.

But that only made things worse.

Amp bobbed his head. He circled his arm. Then he brought the plastic guitar up to his face and started playing it with his licorice-black tongue.

"Gross!" Malcolm said. He'd have to scrub that controller with a gallon of soap once this song was over.

Things were looking bleak. Amp was winning. The old rocker was about to bring the guitar back down when his hair got caught in the buttons. "Ow!" he cried,

dancing around. "Help!"

Notes kept flying by on the screen, but Amp was too busy trying to free his feathery locks. The more he tried to unwind it, the more it got twisted.

Dandy went back into his power stance as the big finish approached. His score inched higher and higher, and just as the last long *waa-waa* of the electric guitar sounded, Dandy's total had rolled up to 150,000 points. Far ahead of Amp's.

"Yes!" Dandy shouted, jumping up and down.

"No fair," Amp whined, his hair a big knot on the guitar neck. He pulled hard, ripping out a big hunk and leaving a glowing bald spot on the side of his head.

"Seriously, dude," Malcolm said, "you have got to stop playing guitar with your

tongue. It never works out for you."

Amp reached up and touched his scalp. His lip poked out as he pouted, "My beautiful hair."

Dandy grinned. "Maybe you should get a cap. But you have to put POR on it. Prince of Rock." His face split into a big grin. "'Cause I'm the king."

Amp sighed and slumped.

"And you better keep your promise," Malcolm warned. "No more terrorizing the arena. 'Cause if it happens again, I won't miss with my zapper."

"I promise," Amp said. Then with a sad puppy look on his face, he vanished.

Ghost Stalkers

Malcolm watched the news every night. It had been two weeks and not one ballerina in *Swan Lake* had pirouetted out of control or danced on tiptoe to "Unraveled." He figured Amp must be gone for good.

Dandy showed up on Saturday afternoon, holding his backpack on one shoulder.

"Check it out," he said to Malcolm as he removed his cap. There were short

stubbles on the side of his head where the bald spot used to be.

Malcolm smiled. "Hey, it's growing back."

"Think Amp's will grow back?" Dandy asked.

"Probably not. He's a ghost," Malcolm explained.

Dandy shrugged. "Oh well." He dropped his backpack to the floor and unzipped it.

"What have you got there?" Malcolm asked.

"I did a lot of extra chores around the house," Dandy told Malcolm. "So Dad took me to Games Aflame. Look what he bought me." He pulled out Ghost Stalkers—the Home Game.

Malcolm couldn't help but be a little jealous. He reached out toward the game. "Man, that's the game I wanted."

"I know," Dandy said, handing it over. "Let's trade." He nodded toward the Rock Like a Star box in the corner.

"Really?" Malcolm asked. He couldn't believe it!

"Yeah," Dandy said. "You're a lot better at ghost hunting than I am. And I can't stay the King of Rock without practice."

"That's true," Malcolm agreed. He grabbed the Ghost Stalkers game and ripped into the package. He was just fine with getting rid of Rock Like a Star.

"Want to play?" Malcolm asked.

"Will it be as much fun as hunting real ghosts?" Dandy asked.

Malcolm shook his head. "Come on, Dandy. You know that nothing is more fun than hunting real ghosts."

Sometimes, ghost detectors need to know how to speak the languages of different ghosts! Here are four rocker phrases that came in handy for Malcolm and Dandy.

1. fret - one of the ridges on the fingerboard of a stringed instrument, such as a guitar.

2. jam - an informal performance by musicians.

3. King of Rock - a nickname for someone who can play rock-and-roll music.

4. power stance - the way a guitar player stands, with feet shoulder-length apart, knees slighty bent, and ready to play.